Growing Up in
Brazil

Other titles in the *Growing Up Around the World* series include:

Growing Up in
Brazil

John Allen

San Diego, CA

© 2018 ReferencePoint Press, Inc.
Printed in the United States

For more information, contact:
ReferencePoint Press, Inc.
PO Box 27779
San Diego, CA 92198
www.ReferencePointPress.com

LIBRARY OF CONGRESS CATALOGING-IN-PUBLICATION DATA

Name: Allen, John, 1957– author.
Title: Growing Up in Brazil/by John Allen.
Description: San Diego, CA: ReferencePoint Press, Inc., [2018] | Series:
  Growing Up Around the World series | Audience: Grade 9 to 12. | Includes
  bibliographical references and index.
Identifiers: LCCN 2017017980 (print) | LCCN 2017023703 (ebook) | ISBN
  9781682822067 (eBook) | ISBN 9781682822050 (hardback)
Subjects: LCSH: Brazil—Social conditions. | Brazil—Economic conditions. |
  Brazil—Religion. | Brazil—Description and travel.
Classification: LCC HN283.5 (ebook) | LCC HN283.5 .A724 2018 (print) | DDC
  306.0981--dc23
LC record available at https://lccn.loc.gov/2017017980

CONTENTS

Venezuela
Guyana
French Guiana
Suriname
ATLANTIC OCEAN
Colombia
Ecuador
Pico da Neblina
Amazon River
Peru
BRAZIL
Brasília
Bolivia
Rio de Janeiro
São Paulo
Chile
Paraguay
PACIFIC OCEAN
Porto Alegre
Argentina
Uruguay
ATLANTIC OCEAN

Rain forest
Pampas
Pantanal
Andes mountains

Official Name
Federative Republic of Brazil

Capital
Brasília

Size
3,287,957 square miles
(8,515,770 sq. km)

Total Population
211,081,141

Youth Population
0–14 years: 22.79%
15–24 years: 16.43%

Religion
Roman Catholic: 64.6%; other Catholic:
0.4%; Protestant: 22.2%; other
Christian: 0.7%; Spiritist: 2.2%; other:
1.4%; none: 8%; unspecified: 0.4%

Type of Government
Federal presidential republic

Language
Portuguese (99%), plus 210
indigenous languages

Currency
Brazilian real

Industries
Textiles, shoes, chemicals, cement,
lumber, iron ore, tin, steel, aircraft,
motor vehicles and parts, other
machinery and equipment

Literacy
92.6% (age 15+ able
to read and write)

Internet Users
120.676 million, or 59.1%
of population

CHAPTER ONE

A Rich Cultural Mix

Kids in the Brazilian city of São Paulo dress like young people in any number of nations—the same jeans, T-shirts, skirts, and blouses found at stores in the mall. But Rafael Varandas, founder of the hip fashion label Cotton Project, wants to offer them clothing that expresses the mixture of cultures—indigenous, African, and European—that makes Brazil such a special place. "Kids are more globalized these days," says Varandas, "they know how the kids in Barcelona, east London and Williamsburg dress and they want to consume all this. So there's been some new brands like Cotton Project that believe in a more open Brazilian couture [fashion], something that connects us to all the foreign culture we've been absorbing all these years."[1] Artistically inclined young people like Varandas see the large cityscapes of Brazil as canvases to be filled with all the color and excitement of a vibrant nation filled with promise.

A Large and Diverse Country

Brazil is the largest country in South America and the fifth largest in the world. Nearly half of all people in South America live in Brazil. It encompasses a total area of 3,287,957 square miles (8,515,770 sq. km), of which more than 19,305 square miles (50,000 sq. km) is water. Brazil extends from the basin of the Amazon River in the north to the vineyards, canyons, and majestic waterfalls of the south. Its long coastline to the east borders the Atlantic Ocean. To the north and northwest are the countries of French Guiana, Suriname, Guyana, Venezuela, and Colombia. Peru, Bolivia, Paraguay, and Argentina lie along the western border, with Uruguay to the south. Brazil also includes islands in the Atlantic Ocean, such as Arquipélago de Fernando de Noronha, a chain of twenty-one islands located about 217 miles (350 km) from the shoreline of Pernambuco. Dolphin Bay in Fernando de Noronha is one of the most beautiful inlets in the world.

Brazil's large size means that it has a number of different climate regions. The zone near the equator sees humidity and rainfall year-round, with no winter season or dry period to speak of. Coastal areas on plateaus mostly experience cool summers and

A young São Paulo woman skateboards down a city street with her dog. Kids in São Paulo dress and behave like kids in many other parts of the world.

warm winters with uniform rainfall throughout the year. Low-lying coastal cities, however, experience very hot summers. Cities on the central plateau are milder in temperature and alternate between humid and dry conditions. Southern regions can be fairly wet and temperate, averaging below 68°F (20°C) in annual median temperature, although some areas get surprisingly cold in winter.

Though it is best known for its dense rain forests, Brazil actually contains a diverse landscape, the extremes of which are familiar to every Brazilian schoolchild. There are fertile grasslands to the south called pampas, the setting of countless adventure tales about gauchos, the swaggering, often mixed-race cowboys of nineteenth-century Brazil. There are also rough hills, large plateaus in the country's central region, pine forests, wetlands, and a long coastal plain. The Brazilian highlands in the northeast feature a series of mountain ranges that separate the country's interior from the Atlantic Ocean. Brazil's highest point—at nearly 9,842 feet (3,000 m) above sea level—is Pico da Neblina, a peak in the Guiana Highlands to the north of the Amazon. The Pantanal in the mideastern section is the largest freshwater wetland on Earth, more than ten times as large as Florida's Everglades.

The Amazon Rain Forest

The tropical rain forest in Brazil's northwest region is the largest in the world, making up an area of 2,123,562 square miles (5,500,000 sq. km) that extends into Colombia, Peru, Bolivia, and other countries. The thick growth of broad-leafed trees and plants covers a huge basin, which is drained by the Amazon River, reputed to be the world's longest at more than 4,000 miles (6,400 km). Besides the tropical rain forest, the area includes other ecosystems, such as natural savannas (mixed woodlands and grasslands) and swamps. Instead of roads and bridges, the Amazon and its network of thousands of tributaries provide navigation through the dense jungle. During the wet season, the Amazon widens in places to more than 120 miles (190 km).

No Brazilian childhood is complete without Amazonian tales of river-dwelling piranha, meat-eating fish, or anacondas, the huge snakes that await unwary travelers in the shallow waters of the Amazon basin. The rain forest is home to an amazing variety of

The white-whiskered spider monkey (shown) is just one of more than four hundred species of mammal that haunt the Brazilian rain forests. These forests teem with even more insect, plant, and bird species.

plant and animal life, perhaps as much as 30 percent of Earth's total species. Plant species alone number more than forty thousand. There are also more than thirteen hundred different kinds of birds, including the blue-bellied parrot and the crescent-chested puffbird; more than four hundred mammals, from the white-whiskered spider monkey to the maned sloth; nearly four hundred reptiles; and close to three thousand species of freshwater fish. Plants and animals in the rain forest exist in a complex relationship in which they depend on each other for survival.

As Brazilian children learn in school, the rain forest plays a major role in keeping the planet healthy. It absorbs carbon dioxide and produces oxygen in vast amounts. It also helps keep the world's climate stable. Yet warming temperatures, population growth, and the drive to modernize Brazil have had a damaging effect on the rain forest. Huge areas have been cleared to make way for agriculture and development—an estimated 18 million acres (7,284,342 ha) are lost every year. This so-called deforestation releases enormous amounts of stored carbon into the atmosphere. Environmental groups are working to educate the public and curb the logging and farming operations that have leveled large swathes of the rain forest. Gisele Bündchen, the Brazilian-born fashion model, recalls learning about the rain forest at school in southern Brazil. "As a child, I grew up thinking this rainforest is this magical place," she says. "Just untouched and it can never be destroyed. And then you grow up and realize, wait a minute, it's actually not indestructible. People are cutting it down to profit from its resources in so many different ways."[2]

> "As a child, I grew up thinking this rainforest is this magical place. Just untouched and it can never be destroyed. And then you grow up and realize, wait a minute, it's actually not indestructible."[2]
>
> —Gisele Bündchen, a Brazilian-born fashion model

The Portuguese and Slavery

Much of Brazil's history deals with those who have sought to profit from its people and resources. Civilizations dating to around eight thousand years ago are believed to have stemmed from people who migrated from Asia by crossing the Pacific Ocean or Bering Strait. These people created pottery, cleared plots of rain forest for farming, and made clever use of forest resources. In 1500, when sailors from Portugal, led by Pedro Álvars Cabral, arrived on the shores of Rio Buranhém, they were met by indigenous people offering peaceful gifts of headwear made from parrot feathers. The Portuguese set about converting the native population to Catholicism. They also established colonies to produce sugarcane and other valuable crops.

When large numbers of native Brazilians fled to the land's interior to avoid slavery and outbreaks of disease, the Portuguese settlers imported slave labor from Africa. Thus, the major influences on Brazil came together soon after colonization, with Europeans, Africans, and indigenous people all contributing cultural elements. Mixed marriages among the races were much more commonplace in Brazil than anywhere else in the world. As a result, most Brazilians share a mixture of bloodlines and take for granted a cultural legacy that is very diverse.

Slavery in Brazil lasted longer and was spread over a larger area than anywhere else in the world. Historians estimate that during the slavery period, which lasted more than three hundred years, nearly 5 million Africans were captured and brought to the country as slaves—ten times more than were trafficked to North America. At the same time, more than six hundred thousand Portuguese immigrated as settlers. In 1822 Dom Pedro, the young prince regent of Portugal, proclaimed Brazil's independence. Yet it was not until 1888 that slavery was abolished in Brazil, and the state did little to help former slaves find their place in society. "Even today, the vast majority of Brazilians of African origin remain at the bottom of Brazil's social pyramid," says Thiago de Paula Souza of the Afro-Brazilian Museum. "The difference between whites and blacks are obvious when considering police violence, life expectancy, access to public services (such as health and education), earning capacity, and unemployment figures."[3]

More than 53 percent of Brazilians today consider themselves black or of mixed African ancestry. Brazilians have long had the reputation of being virtually blind to racial differences, but some newcomers dispute this claim. One young black woman from London, who came to Brazil when her husband got a job there, admits she was disappointed with how she was received. "My skin is very dark," she says, "so going out with my children, on occasions people would say to me, 'Are you the nanny for these children?' And I'd have to explain to them, no, these are my children, I look after them."[4]

Economic and social disparity among races affects daily life in many ways. Some children feel the difference at an early age. "My 3-year-old has started to come home from school, and he's started to rub my arms and my skin," says the young woman from London. "He'd say, 'Mummy, I'm trying to get the brown off.'"[5] Black youth in Brazil also face a shortage of jobs and constant danger from violence. Statistics show that young Afro-Brazilians are murdered at the rate of one every twenty-three minutes. To combat racial prejudice, the Brazilian government has begun a program called *discriminação positiva*, or "positive discrimination," which is much like affirmative action in the United States.

An Uncertain Economy

Along with race-related issues, Brazil has struggled with government corruption. Brazil's form of government is a democratic republic, with its president elected to a four-year term and eligible for reelection to a second term. Voting is required for Brazilian residents between ages eighteen and sixty-nine. Sixteen- and seventeen-year-olds are also able to vote if they choose, as are those who are seventy and over. The national capital in Brasília, located in the central highlands, oversees twenty-six states and the federal district of Brasília. Civilian rule is important in a country that has experienced turbulent changes over the years. In 1964 Brazil's military seized power from a leftist regime, and a series of generals ruled the country for two decades. Not until 1989 were Brazilians able to vote directly for a president in a national election.

Years of turmoil left the nation with a failing economy. In the late 1990s Brazil had to rely on loans from the International Monetary Fund to avoid financial collapse. The government spent billions on antipoverty programs to provide health care and education for children. In 2002 Brazilians elected Luiz Inácio Lula da Silva of the Worker's Party as president. During his two terms, Lula (as he is known), a former factory worker and labor organizer, managed to turn the economy around, lifted more than 20 million Brazilians out of poverty, and became enormously popular. However, Dilma Rousseff, Lula's chosen successor, was removed from office in September 2016 on corruption charges, and the economy has been shrinking at an alarming rate—3.6 percent in 2016. Inflation hovers at more than 10 percent, which saps family savings. Young Brazilians today worry about finding good jobs in such an uncertain environment.

Despite recent setbacks, Brazil has the ninth-largest economy in the world and the largest in Latin America. The service sector, including banking and tourism, makes up two-thirds of the economy, with manufacturing responsible for another 28 percent. Agriculture accounts for only a small fraction of Brazil's economic output. Petrobras, a Brazilian oil and gas company, is the world's fourth-largest corporation, but it too has been caught up in the corruption scandal, and falling oil prices have contributed to the downturn.

Although Lula's policies helped improve income inequality in Brazil, there are still large gaps in income between different segments of society, with the urban and rural poor still struggling to survive. The issue of jobs and income inequality is especially urgent for the youth of Brazil. "The people who will manage the

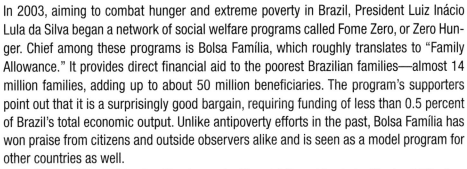

An Antipoverty Program That Works

In 2003, aiming to combat hunger and extreme poverty in Brazil, President Luiz Inácio Lula da Silva began a network of social welfare programs called Fome Zero, or Zero Hunger. Chief among these programs is Bolsa Família, which roughly translates to "Family Allowance." It provides direct financial aid to the poorest Brazilian families—almost 14 million families, adding up to about 50 million beneficiaries. The program's supporters point out that it is a surprisingly good bargain, requiring funding of less than 0.5 percent of Brazil's total economic output. Unlike antipoverty efforts in the past, Bolsa Família has won praise from citizens and outside observers alike and is seen as a model program for other countries as well.

Bolsa Família provides families in need with a debit card loaded with about fifty-four dollars a month. Usually the money goes to the family's mother. The funds are used to buy food, clothing, medicine, and other necessities. To receive the payments, families must make sure that children are in school and have been vaccinated. In fact, one of the program's main goals is to keep children in school and subject to better health care. "Poverty is concentrated on children; they were unprotected," says Luis Henrique Paiva, a Brazilian social worker based at the Brooks World Poverty Institute. "If they have better access to education and healthcare they will probably have a better prospect. Both in the short and the long term we could do something for these children, using cash transfers."

Quoted in Sarah Illingworth, "Bolsa Família: The Program Helping 50M Brasilians to Exit Poverty," *Huffington Post*, June 10, 2015. www.huffingtonpost.com.

country for the next two years have a great responsibility towards young Brazilians," says business executive Paolo Dal Pino, referring to the government's proposals for new jobs programs. "If they don't do what we hope they will do, we will lose 10 years."[6]

Life in the Cities

Issues related to young people loom large because they make up such a large percentage of the population. Of Brazil's 211 million people, nearly 40 percent are under age twenty-four, with about 23 percent under age fourteen. There is constant demand for better schools and more job opportunities for the young. Yet it is the youth of Brazil who provide a strong sense of optimism about the future.

As in most developing countries, the people of Brazil are moving to urban areas. This can lead to overpopulation and a strain on public services. The largest cities are on the southeast coast, including São Paulo with a population of 12 million and Rio de Janeiro with more than 6 million. The capital city of Brasília, located in the interior, contains 2.2 million people. In 2015 the rural population stood at about 30 million, a drop of more than 10 million since its height in 1974.

> "The people who will manage the country for the next two years have a great responsibility towards young Brazilians. If they don't do what we hope they will do, we will lose 10 years."[6]
>
> —Brazilian business executive Paolo Dal Pino

Daily life in the big coastal cities offers a panorama of recreation and culture—a quality of excitement and hubbub that Brazilians call *movimento*. Upper- and middle-class youth can enjoy beautiful beaches, manicured parks, streets lined with glittering skyscrapers, upscale malls and shopping areas, movie theaters, concert halls, and stadiums that feature world-class matches in soccer—or *futebol*, as Brazilians call the sport that is their national passion. Recent city ordinances in São Paulo and elsewhere have allowed more food trucks on the street, serving delicious food curbside. (Although youth in Brazil, obeying a cultural norm, mostly resist touching food with their bare hands.) Brazilians in their teens and even younger are as obsessed with their cell phones as are young people the world over. A 2011

These Rio de Janeiro youths enjoy diving into the warm blue water from this ledge near one of the many white-sand beaches the city offers. Brazil's coastal cities afford citizens a wide array of cultural and sporting events to attend and participate in—an active lifestyle they term movimento.

survey by Trend Micro, an Internet security firm, noted that Brazil had the world's highest percentage of children with smartphones at 27 percent. And children in Brazil were joining social networking sites at the average age of nine, which was much younger than in most countries. Young Brazilians love to share the latest gossip about music, clothes, celebrities, and television favorites such as the hugely popular *telenovelas*, or soap operas. The corruption scandals that have rocked the nation are mostly just background noise to young people focused on their friends, family, and schoolwork.

Urban and Rural Poverty

Brazilian cities, however, offer a stark contrast between rich and poor. For the less fortunate, daily life can be a constant struggle. In Rio de Janeiro, one of the world's most glamorous tourist destinations, poor families live crowded together in hillside shantytowns called *favelas*. These makeshift neighborhoods, often lacking basic services, date from the end of slavery in the late 1800s, when freed slaves sought cheap housing. The favelas spread rapidly with the movement of poor rural families to the city between 1940 and 1970. Today life in the favelas is marked by drug use, threats of violence, and crushing poverty. With parents or single mothers toiling away at menial jobs, kids gather in small groups to kick around a soccer ball or smoke marijuana. (In Brazil, possession of small amounts of marijuana is illegal but punished only with a warning and a brief term of community service.)

Eleven-year-old twins Samira and Samir da Silva live in Complexo da Mare, one of Rio's most notorious favelas. Their mother forbids them to play in the street for fear of gangs, guns, and drunk drivers. Instead, they kick a ball together in a tiny enclosed

Dreams of a Career in Soccer

On a typical Sunday, the dirt lots next to the favelas in Rio de Janeiro are filled with kids playing soccer. They try to copy the moves of their heroes on the national team, controlling the ball and weaving their way through defenders with great skill. Children as young as seven already have a special feel for the game. "For every 10 kids in Brazil, 11 of them want to be a professional soccer player," jokes Renato Deasevedo, a youth soccer coach. Brazil's reputation as a hotbed of soccer talent lures international scouts looking for the next Pelé or Ronaldo, two of the nation's most revered players. In their teens, the best young players can sign contracts with European clubs for huge sums. Brazil has been described as a football factory, exporting soccer talent for high-paying jobs around the world.

Unfortunately, these opportunities exist only for males. Although soccer is very popular among Brazilian girls, there is not the same infrastructure and investment for them as there is for boys. The discrepancy reaches all the way to the upper levels of the sport. Daiane Rodrigues, a star on Brazil's national team, would probably be quite wealthy if she were male, but instead she must supplement her income by selling ice cream at her town's soccer stadium. Brazilian soccer officials say the differences are due to cultural resistance to women in sport.

Quoted in Christof Putzel, "Brazil's Football Factory: Supplying the Global Demand for Talent," *Aljazeera America*, June 23, 2014. http://america.aljazeera.com.

cement patio. Frequent shootings near their school often result in canceled classes and more idle time for the children. Police raids in their neighborhood are commonplace. "Sometimes we go three days without classes," says Samir. "We stay home then. There's nothing we can do about it."[7]

Life in villages and rural areas can also be harsh. (In Brazil, to say one lives in the interior implies a rural address.) Some people in these areas toil on their own small farms and live in two-room houses built of stone or adobe. Many work on large ranches, plantations, or cooperatives. It is possible to make a good living growing cash crops such as coffee, sugarcane, and soybeans. Besides doing chores, some rural youths are learning about new technologies for farming, such as drones for checking crops and automated systems for irrigation. Nonetheless, farm life can be hard, with so much depending on good weather and adequate rainfall. For example, in the rural dry lands of the northeast interior, poverty and malnutrition are all too common.

A Cultural Melting Pot

Wherever they live, Brazilian youth tend to absorb the rich mixture of cultures in their country. Almost all Brazilians speak Portuguese, a language similar to, but distinct from, Spanish. A Brazilian learns as a child to resent the frequent assumption by foreigners that she or he speaks Spanish. Portuguese, as spoken in Brazil, has also added many terms from the nation's indigenous languages, such as words for plants, animals, and places. African influence is found everywhere, such as in dishes served in Bahia in northeast Brazil. These include *vatapá,* a spicy seafood stew, and *acarajé,* which are fritters made with black-eyed peas. World-famous musical forms, including samba and bossa nova (meaning "the new thing"), incorporate lilting African rhythms with European harmonies. One example of Brazil's cultural melting pot is found during Carnival, which is the Catholic celebration marking the beginning of Lent, the forty-day period before Easter. Floats and costumes are decorated with brightly colored feathers and ornaments based on native Brazilian designs, and while bands play African-based music, dancers gyrate to tribal rhythms. The event embodies the vibrant combination of cultures that young Brazilians learn to embrace as their heritage.

CHAPTER TWO

Family Life

When Susana Raysa de Carvalho gets home from school each day, she always receives a kiss from her father, Roberto. Susana, sixteen, shares a room in the family's small apartment with her twenty-two-year-old sister, Sandra. Their working-class neighborhood in the northeastern city of Recife is shabby but respectable. Life can be hard getting by on Roberto's modest salary as a truck mechanic. Both Roberto and his wife, Enilda, a talented seamstress, migrated to the city to escape the grinding poverty of farm life in rural Brazil. Roberto grew up without electricity or running water.

Today the Carvalhos pride themselves on having reached the lower rungs of the middle class in Recife. A recent promotion enabled Roberto to purchase smartphones for his daughters, a microwave oven, and a flat-screen television. The Carvalhos form a tight family unit, encouraging each other's dreams for the future. One major goal is to trade their tiny apartment for a full-size house—an investment that will require a sum of $40,000. "I think that's our task now," says Sandra, who works as a nurse. "That's a dream of mine. And I'm definitely going to reach it."[8]

The Importance of Family

The close-knit Carvalhos are an example of how the family remains the bedrock of Brazilian society. The importance of the family unit follows from the way Brazilians focus more on collective values than on individual ones. Interaction with family members and close friends comes as naturally as breathing to most Brazilians. A home in Brazil is generally filled with lots of activity and the sounds of bubbling talk and laughter. Everyone joins in on the conversation, from kids to grandparents. The idea of needing time to oneself is quite foreign to most Brazilians. Many see solitude as a sign of unhappiness or depression.

In Brazil, the bond between parent and child is very strong. Children are brought up to respect their parents and obey them always. By the same token, parental love is expressed in values of concern, acceptance, and forgiveness. Each child usually receives two surnames at birth—the mother's and the father's—reflecting a lifelong bond with the families of both parents. When a Brazilian child talks about family, he or she generally means an extended group of relatives, not just the nuclear family of parents and offspring.

Children are treated as important members of the family from an early age, and they are included in most activities just like the adults. This attitude toward children helps create an atmosphere of mutual support in the home and encourages young people to

A Brazilian mother and daughter pose for a photo at the beach. Brazilian parents have a strong bond with their children.

develop self-confidence. They also help with caring for infants and toddlers. A baby is not simply relegated to a crib or carriage but instead is cuddled and entertained while family life swirls around in an uproar. It is likely that this early approach to child care is what makes young Brazilians so comfortable around large groups of people.

Another responsibility is checking on older relatives. Emphasis on family ties means that elderly family members rarely are placed in nursing homes or assisted-care facilities. Instead, they occupy an important place in the home as a source of advice and stories about family history. Children in the household are expected to help a grandparent by bringing a cold drink or finding a misplaced pair of glasses. In turn, elderly relatives often delight in helping out

The Tragedy of Street Children

In Brazil today are thousands of homeless children who live on the street and fall prey to drugs, violence, disease, and malnutrition. These street children come from poor families who have either abandoned them completely or prefer only minimal contact. Some have escaped a violent parent; others have followed the example of peers and have become hooked on drugs. Some, referred to as "children of the closed latch," make failed attempts to keep in touch with their families. Poverty leads others to quit school and find some way to make money. Parents of street children generally have little education and often are unemployed. Male children more often wind up on the street, outnumbering females by a ratio of nine to one. Roaming the poorest parts of cities, sleeping in parking garages or alleyways, eating scraps from garbage cans, the street children struggle to survive from day to day.

In a nation that prides itself on close-knit families, the plight of street children is all the more tragic. They are even found wandering the streets of wealthy neighborhoods of large cities like Rio de Janeiro. Before the 2016 Summer Olympic Games, police in Rio tried to hide this problem from visiting journalists and photographers. However, advocates for the homeless opposed this face-saving effort. "They're trying to give the image that Brazil is safe, that we are nice, that we are happy, that everything is all right," said Daniel Medeiros, an advocate for street children. "But it's just a big lie."

Quoted in Michael Kaplan, "Road to Rio: Police Sweep Away 'Street Children' Ahead of Brazil Olympics," *International Business Times*, April 18, 2016. www.ibtimes.com.

the youngsters. "I like my two grandmothers," says Jaqueline, an eight-year-old whose family lives in São Paulo. "But I like the one I live with [her maternal grandmother] most. Because I know what she does for me. She does me loads of favors."[9]

Brazilian society as a whole offers special treatment for seniors. All private businesses and government facilities are required to give priority to those aged sixty and over. This allows seniors to use special lines at the bank, post office, and supermarket.

Support from the *Parentela*

Some families continue to have three generations all living together—often to share living expenses. Brazilians have long had a special name for this extended family—the *parentela*. It consists of the nuclear family plus aunts, uncles, cousins, in-laws, and even godparents (called *padrinhos*). If not under the same roof, relatives often live close together in the neighborhood, sometimes in apartments in the same building. Longtime friends also form a valued part of the *parentela*. In wealthier families, even servants and household workers are welcomed into the fold. In many ways the *parentela* takes the place of social gatherings in churches, country clubs, cultural circles, social clubs, and support groups that exist in the United States and other countries.

> "They have a joy for life in Brazil unlike any country I've ever seen."[10]
>
> —Brazilian-born actress Morena Baccarin

Grown children generally live at home until they are married. Newlyweds who leave to set up their own household not only keep close ties to their parents but also to their extended family. This is natural since relationships with the *parentela* go back to childhood. A Brazilian child grows up seeing his or her aunts and uncles every day and socializes with them on weekends and holidays. Although modern life has weakened some of the *parentela* ties, family unity remains important. A seventy-five-year study at Harvard University found that the Brazilian emphasis on family led to increased happiness and good health. As Brazilian-born actress Morena Baccarin insists, "They have a joy for life in Brazil unlike any country I've ever seen."[10]

Families spend a great deal of time together, working, playing, arguing, and gossiping. The members of the family learn to depend on each other at all times. Having so many family members around gives Brazilian children a sense of stability and emotional warmth. Great importance is placed on being loyal to family members. If a child or adolescent needs help or advice, he or she can go to anyone in the extended family.

Home Life

Another way family members support each other is by sharing household chores. Children in Brazil are expected to pitch in and help with cooking, cleaning, and doing laundry. Along with schoolwork, this ensures that they are rarely idle. Some Brazilian families still divide household duties according to gender, with the mother supervising the children and managing the housework while the husband handles the budget and repairs. As teenager Danika Oliver notes, "I can't say much about all men in Brazil, but I can tell about my dad and my brother. My house [has] some kind of not spoken patriarchal system, my dad 'tells' (mumbles) to me and my mom that something is dirty or messed in the house, then if my mom is already in charge of [some] other task, it is my time to go there and clean."[11]

> "My house [has] some kind of not spoken patriarchal system, my dad 'tells' (mumbles) to me and my mom that something is dirty or messed in the house, then if my mom is already in charge of [some] other task, it is my time to go there and clean."[11]
>
> —Danika Oliver, a teenager in Brazil

Danika admits that her father's attitude toward so-called woman's work gets under her skin, and her brother often takes over the task to avoid a row. But more men today are willing to do their share of household work besides just maintenance and repairs, providing an example for boys in the family to follow.

Traditionally, the male is the head of the household and main breadwinner in Brazil. Men are used to being in control both in public and private life. They often see their role as being the necessary protectors of women. However, with the recent strides women have made, many families now have both spouses earning salaries. Men used to make all the important family decisions themselves, but most women now expect to share this responsibility. With Brazilian women becoming better educated and working at higher-paying jobs, their status in the family is changing as well. These changes promise to strengthen the family unit and provide role models for children to follow.

Leisure Time

When chores are done and there is time to relax, Brazilian kids do many of the same things as children around the world. Video games are extremely popular, even among very young children. They love to watch cartoons and kids' shows on television. Children in Brazil typically love music, listening to both American tunes and the homegrown variety. Xuxa (pronounced *Shoo-sha*), a Brazilian singer, is known as *Rainha dos Baizinhos* (Queen of the Kids). She has recorded a number of catchy songs that are very popular with children. Among other pastimes, kids play the guitar, paint and draw pictures, fly kites, race toy slot cars called Autorama, kick around the soccer ball, and play all sorts of games,

Brazilian boys hone their soccer skills on a city street corner. Kids in Brazil enjoy the same pastimes as kids everywhere.

including tag and hide-and-seek. By middle school, young Brazilians are often so busy with schoolwork and organized activities like sports or music that they interact with their parents for only a few minutes a day during meals.

Mealtimes

Even with the faster pace of modern life, family meals hold a special place in Brazilian culture. "Mealtimes in Brazil are usually an event for family and friends," writes food blogger Rosana McPhee. "There's always plenty of food for late or unexpected arrivals. It's the time of day to catch up and share special moments with loved ones."[12] On school days breakfast tends to be quick and simple. Children drink juice or a cup of milky coffee and eat tropical fruit such as mangoes and papayas, bread with butter and jam, or a grilled ham and cheese sandwich. Kids who walk to school might stop at a street stall for a *coxinha*, a crunchy deep-fried chicken snack.

> "Mealtimes in Brazil are usually an event for family and friends. There's always plenty of food for late or unexpected arrivals. It's the time of day to catch up and share special moments with loved ones."[12]
>
> —Food blogger Rosana McPhee

When the family gathers on weekends or holidays, lunch is the biggest meal of the day. Dishes are generally prepared from scratch with great care. Everyone from small children to grandparents is expected to crowd around the table and make time for an extended midday meal with multiple courses. "Now, here's a Brazilian custom I miss enormously: a decent, sit-down, leisurely-paced lunch and/or dinner," says Sheila Thomson, an expert on Brazilian culture. "To this day, I have to keep reminding myself 'What's the big hurry?' and I confess that one of the things I look forward to, when I go to Brazil, are the 'family' meals."[13] Lunch is a hearty mix of beef dishes, rice and beans, *queijo coalho* (grilled cheese on a stick), and salad. *Feijoada*, a thick stew of meat and black beans, also is served regularly. The children cannot wait to get to dessert and the national favorite, *brigadeiros*, which are balls of condensed milk and cocoa powder dipped in butter and rolled in chocolate sprinkles. Parents know there is risk of a rambunctious

A Multicultural Stew

One symbol of Brazilian hospitality—and its multicultural heritage—is a steaming pot of *feijoada*, a distinctive black bean stew. Recipes for feijoada, which means "big bean," date back to slavery days. Reportedly Brazilian slaves invented the stew as a way to make use of leftovers from the household's table. They would add discarded parts of a pig, such as ears, nose, tail, and feet. They also included the large black beans set aside for their daily meals to make a thick, black, hearty concoction.

Over time feijoada came to include other ingredients, such as sausage from the Portuguese and a toasted manioc flour called *farofa* from native Brazilians. This multicultural blend of cuisines suited ranchers and field laborers who needed energy for a long day's work. Feijoada soon began to appear in fine restaurants, served traditionally on Wednesdays and Saturdays. Today a family will prepare a pot of feijoada at the beginning of a long weekend and add extra meat, beans, and spices at intervals. This ensures that the thick, black stew tastes a bit different from meal to meal. Often it is served with sliced oranges, chopped greens, rice, and a peppery onion sauce. For many young Brazilians, the aroma of feijoada simmering on the stove or over an open fire reminds them of home and family life. "Today there is not just one recipe for Feijoada," says the historian Rodrigo Elias. "On the contrary, it seems to be a dish still in creation."

Rodrigo Elias, "Feijoada: A Short History of an Edible Institution," Cultural Department of Itamaraty. http://dc.itamaraty .gov.br.

sugar high, but they also recall how much they loved the chocolate balls when they were young. After a long afternoon of eating and loud talk, children and adults alike are ready for a relaxing siesta.

Dinner is a much lighter affair, featuring soup, bread, and perhaps some cold cuts. It is also served quite late in the day, as late as nine o'clock. At the beginning and end of meals, Brazilians typically have a small cup of coffee—extremely strong for adults, diluted with milk for older children. Brazilian kids learn table manners for extended meals at an early age. If a family dines out at a restaurant, the children are expected to follow the proper etiquette. They are taught to eat with the fork in left hand, the knife in right, and to almost never pick up food with their fingers.

Families in Brazil love to entertain guests and friends and are generous with food and drinks, even when they live modestly themselves. Visitors to the country often remark on Brazilians' natural hospitality. A party or celebration may be planned on the slightest pretext. When the World Cup was held in Brazil in 2014 and the Summer Olympics in 2016, Brazilian families organized huge parties to watch the games on television. Fans from every part of the world were welcomed into watch parties and offered an ice-cold beer or *caipirinha*, a cocktail made from a sugarcane-based hard liquor. Birthdays, graduations, and promotions also call for food and revelry. Young couples hold a *chá de revelação*, which is a party to reveal the sex of an unborn baby. Families in coastal cities love to set up beach parties with a bonfire, lots of food, music, and dancing. Separate groups soon mingle together in one large celebration. As with all family activities, children from teens to toddlers are expected to join in.

Rural Families

Family life in rural Brazil also has its joys but is often marked by hardship. One in four people in rural areas lives in poverty. Most of the more than 5 million farms in Brazil are family owned and very small. During recent hard times, particularly in the dry northeast, poverty rates among these farms and ranches have risen to more than 60 percent. Farm families often lack access to good health care and education, and they struggle to support themselves with variable crops. Even finding enough water to use can be a problem. As one young Brazilian woman in rural Bahia reports:

> Our water ran out, and we gamely soldiered on for a few days. We conserved. We used water that we brought by the gallon from town (which also is starting to have shortages and rations in the afternoon). We talked to the municipality about bringing their water truck to refill our cistern and they turned us down—their water is low enough, they said, that they needed to save it for [the] city and couldn't justify trips to the rural zones as they had in the past.[14]

Still, like their Brazilian counterparts in the cities, rural families find strength in solidarity and shared values. Most families in rural Brazil dwell in tiny one- or two-room houses of adobe or stone

A young woman in a poor rural village in Brazil smiles for the camera during her chores. One out of four people in Brazil's rural communities lives in poverty.

with roofs of red clay tiles. Space is at a premium, so furnishings and possessions are few and simple. Children stay busy with chores, such as feeding livestock, caring for babies, or even helping with work in the fields.

Everyone must work long hours, so mealtimes are a welcome break. Meals consist of meat, beans, and vegetables in plain dishes that are quick to prepare. Around the table everyone talks at once. As in the cities and towns, rural kids discuss the latest television stars and popular singers. Not even the difficulties of life on a remote family farm can dampen the spirits of most young Brazilians.

Decreases in Family Size

Traditionally, both rural and urban families in Brazil have been large. However, like the Carvalhos, many Brazilian couples are now having fewer children. The country's birthrate has plummeted from 6.15 children per woman in 1960 to an estimated 1.76 in 2016. The drop is seen everywhere, from São Paulo, with its tiny apartments and hectic lifestyle, to villages in the Amazon and towns in the central farming belt.

> "Before, I wanted four children and had even picked out names. But now I just want one. It's too hard these days; you have to pay for schooling, for health care—there are all kinds of costs."[15]
>
> —Priscila da Silva, a restaurant owner in Rio de Janeiro

Reasons for the decline include increased use of contraceptives, more job opportunities for women, and migration to cities, where raising children is more expensive than in rural areas. Moreover, large numbers of young people are influenced by telenovelas like *Fina Estampa* (*Fine Portrait*), in which characters are rich and glamorous and have few children. Many ambitious young women are deciding to focus on their careers and waiting to have children until age thirty or later. This is a huge change in a Latin American society that still is marked by machismo, or male privilege, and the idea that large families and more people make for a stronger nation. Priscila da Silva, a restaurant owner in Rio whose grandmother had twelve children, admits that she has changed her mind about having a large family. "Before, I wanted four children and had even picked out names," she says. "But now I just want one. It's too hard these days; you have to pay for schooling, for health care—there are all kinds of costs."[15]

Winning legal equality has been a slow process for Brazilian women. They won the right to vote only in 1932. As late as the

1960s women were legally equivalent to children. They could not leave the country or open a bank account without the permission of a spouse or parent. Even today a woman's worth is often measured by her youth and beauty, leading to a thriving industry for plastic surgeons.

But the push for equal rights is beginning to achieve success. Improvement in women's social and economic positions has also brought changes to family structures in Brazil. The nuclear family arrangement of a husband, wife, and children all living under one roof is no longer the overwhelming choice for young people. In 2010 only about 40 percent of Brazilians were officially married. So-called stable unions, in which couples who live together for more than two years are granted legal status as a family, make up 36 percent of the population. About one-fifth of Brazilian families are headed by a single parent, almost always the mother. Divorce, once relatively rare, is now a much easier process to navigate for couples with children. It remains to be seen how these new family arrangements will affect young people in the years to come.

CHAPTER THREE

Education and Employment

For high-school graduates in Brazil who want to attend college, the vestibular is all-important. (The word *vestibular* is a Latin-related term that suggests access to a pathway.) It is the Brazilian equivalent of the SAT, a grueling two- or three-day test with a student's future on the line. Students have nicknamed it "the funnel"[16] for the way it narrows down the applicant pool. For months before the test, students put in hours of study in math, physics, biology, geography, English, and Portuguese. Vacations and friends are put on hold. A number attend yearlong, specialized—and expensive—courses called *cursinhos* that aid in preparation. They know that a good score on the vestibular is vital due to the fierce competition for places at the best colleges and universities. For example, in any given year more than sixty thousand apply to Rio de Janeiro State University, competing for roughly four thousand available spots. Anxiety builds as the date of the vestibular approaches. Failure means a six-month wait for another opportunity, or for those with few resources, abandonment of the dream of higher education. Newspapers publish stories about applicants who got caught in traffic and missed the exam. They also advise parents on how to console students whose scores fall short. According to Sofia Rocha, an eighteen-year-old seeking a degree in industrial design, "You live with tension before the exam, during the exam and then after the exam. It's been so long since I've gone to the beach or to a party that I can barely remember what it's like. For now, I can only hope that when they put up the results, I will finally have a reason to celebrate."[17]

The Brazilian School System

Young Brazilians fret about getting accepted to college because they know education is key to their future. In this way they are dependent on government support for schools. The public school system begins with preschool, a level that includes day care and is called *creche* in Portuguese. Beginning in 2016 preschool became mandatory—and thus government funded—for kids between ages four and six. There are two kinds of preschool. Maternal preschool is a nursery school focused on day care and group play. *Jardim*, for kids ages three to six, is more of a kindergarten, featuring an academic program that also teaches social skills. The school consults with parents to decide which type of preschool is best for their child. *Jardim* programs also seek parent input to address each child's situation and aptitude.

The next stage in the school system, called *ensino fundamental* (fundamental education I and II), is mandatory for students ages six through fourteen. The grade-school level goes from first to fifth grade, and the middle-school level goes from sixth to ninth grade. The high-school level, called *ensino médio*, includes students from ages fifteen to eighteen and goes from tenth to twelfth grade. *Ensino médio* has been mandatory only since 2016.

Usually schools in Brazil, both public and private, mix all academic levels together in the same class. Under the state system, an exam is given at the end of each academic year to determine if a child moves on to the next grade or must repeat a grade. Since repeating a grade is quite common, particularly in public schools, the mixture of ages in a classroom can be varied. Schools in remote areas may have only one large room where students of all ages and grade levels are instructed by a single teacher. Brazilian law also allows for homeschooling, although parents must complete an extensive application process for the right to educate their children at home.

> "You live with tension before the exam, during the exam and then after the exam. It's been so long since I've gone to the beach or to a party that I can barely remember what it's like."[17]
>
> —Sofia Rocha, an eighteen-year-old Brazilian, on taking the vestibular

Brazilian young people, like the students in this São Paulo high school class, recognize that education is the key to a better future. In Brazil, students usually attend school only in a morning or afternoon session each day.

In both public and private schools, school hours for Brazilian children run from 7 a.m. to 11:45 a.m. or from noon to 4:45 p.m. A student attends only one of these sessions per day. Schools offer these different shifts to deal with the great number of students enrolled. Smaller schools, especially in the rural interior, may offer only one daily session for all children. Most rules about school terms and holidays are set by the local government. The federal government has few requirements for schools. Among these are that July must be a holiday month, schools must provide a break at the end of the calendar year, and primary pupils must attend school for at least two hundred days a year. School terms usually go from February to June and from August to December. Summer vacation is in January or February, which are warm months in the Southern Hemisphere.

A Day at School

A typical child in Brazil rises at 6 a.m. to get ready for school. She or he will bolt a breakfast of buns, fruit, and juice before heading out the door. The school day generally begins at 7 a.m. when the class rises to sing "Hino Nacional," the Brazilian national anthem. Many schools require pupils to wear uniforms so that everyone is dressed the same, even though the uniform is often simply a T-shirt featuring the school logo. Schools in Brazil are not segregated by race, but the realities of social status usually mean that schools in wealthy areas include mostly white students. Schools in less affluent districts feature a mixture of black, white, and mixed-race students as a matter of course.

Some teachers in Brazil wear a lab coat that is also emblazoned with the school logo on the pocket. Brazilian teachers are known for addressing their students in a loud voice so that everyone can hear easily. They ask lots of questions and call on individuals regularly to keep the entire class alert. Students remain in one classroom as they tackle different subjects, such as math, geography, science, social studies, and Portuguese. Even upper-level students stay in one place while various teachers rotate through to instruct them in different subjects.

Students receive activity books that contain assignments in all their subjects, allowing them to organize their work in one large book. As each assignment is completed, the teacher grades it and signs the page. Tests are frequent, administered at least once a week, usually on Mondays or Fridays. At wealthier schools, students also use computers to learn computing skills, play educational games, and do additional work. The Brazilian government is committed to providing more computers to schools throughout the nation, but most schools have only one computer per classroom or perhaps two or three for the entire school.

After a while students get a midmorning break, called *intervalo*. Children spend this time eating a school-provided snack and playing games, including tag, hide-and-seek, and singing games. Older students might chat or take part in line dancing. As for organized activities, limited budgets typically keep schools from focusing on nonacademic pursuits, such as sports and instruction in art and music. Students who want to participate in these activities join a sports club or attend classes at a community center.

Short Days and Attendance Problems

The rest of the school day goes by quickly, as morning classes end before noon. The short daily sessions can cause problems regarding what to do with the remainder of the day. Students may hurry home to share the midday meal with their parents and other family members—a longtime Brazilian tradition. Some students get rides from their parents or friends' parents, but others walk home or gather with other children. Thirteen-year-old Andersom Batista de Andrade Jr. makes good use of his afternoons. "I have some time before I go to an after-school center that is close to my home," he says. "It was created by a non-government organization, or NGO, a nonprofit group that created a program for my community. While I'm at the center, I get help with my math lessons and homework."[18] Later Andersom practices capoeira, a form of Brazilian martial arts that mixes self-defense, dance, acrobatics, and music. He also gets in some time on his skateboard before returning home to his mother and sister.

Some schools also offer evening classes for older students from 5 to 10 p.m. Schools that have an evening session often are trying to reduce the dropout rate by accommodating students who must work during the day to help support their families. Attendance continues to be a huge problem in Brazilian schools located in impoverished areas. Struggling parents sometimes encourage children as young as ten to skip school in favor of earning money—despite laws that set the minimum working age at sixteen. Other parents may have school-age children working at home. "Child labor is growing again in many places and affecting the youngest, most vulnerable children," says Jonathan Hannay, secretary-general of ACER Brasil, a charity group that works with at-risk young people in São Paulo. "Much of this is domestic work at home, caused by the staggered, short 'shifts' that Brazilian schools operate for their pupils and by parents having to travel many hours to work each day."[19] It is estimated that some 5 million underaged children in Brazil have left school to work instead.

> "Child labor is growing again in many places and affecting the youngest, most vulnerable children."[19]
>
> —Jonathan Hannay, secretary-general of ACER Brasil

Two young mining workers take a break from their labors. About 5 million such youngsters are estimated to have left school to go to work instead.

Secondary School, College, and Trade School

Students in Brazilian secondary school, or *ensino médio*, concentrate on courses that prepare them for entering a university. Besides the core subjects, these include sociology, philosophy, chemistry, and a foreign language, usually English. Finally it is time to study for the vestibular or the Enem (Exame Nacional do Ensino Médio), the entrance exams for public universities. Passing one of these tests brings each student a huge sense of accomplishment and relief. Since 2009 the Enem has begun to overshadow the vestibular since it allows poorer students to apply at 115 different universities at once. Questions on the Enem can even become a national issue. A recent essay question on the Enem dealt with "the persistence of violence against women in Brazilian society,"[20]

A Scholarship Program for Low-Income Students

Economists in Brazil have long insisted that expanding higher education is the key to boosting social mobility and lifting up the underclasses. The Brazilian government has responded with policies that help poor students attend university. One of the most successful of these is called ProUni (Programa Universidade para Todos), or the University for All Program. ProUni provides university scholarships for students from low-income families, and it pays anywhere from 25 to 100 percent of student expenses. To vie for a full scholarship, each applicant must score higher than 450 points on the Enem entrance exam and affirm that the family's total monthly household income is less than 1.5 times the minimum wage. A scholarship runs for the full time of the university program. To maintain the grant money, each student must pass at least three-quarters of his or her courses per semester. After completing the program, the student has no obligation to pay back the grant money.

More than half of ProUni grants have gone to black or mixed-race students, providing a crucial push for racial equality in higher education. Fernando Rodrigues, who used a ProUni grant to attend university in São Paulo, strongly endorses the program. "My overall experience was good, I received the ProUni financial support throughout my five years of my [course studies] and there was never any trouble," he says. "I just needed to prove my socioeconomic situation every year since it was required, keep my grades above average and sign a statement of commitment annually."

Quoted in Michela DellaMonica, "ProUni Scholarship Recipients Register for 2014 in Brazil," *Rio Times*, July 15, 2014. http://riotimesonline.com.

a topic that some observers criticized as too political but others defended as relevant to today's Brazil.

Oddly enough, public universities in Brazil generally outrank private ones academically—the reverse of the situation for public and private primary schools and secondary schools. This accounts for young Brazilians' drive to get accepted into a public university. Each university year is divided into two semesters. The first semester typically begins in March and lasts until the first of July. The second semester begins in August and ends in mid-December. A bachelor's degree in most fields requires four years of study, and a professional degree takes five years. A medical degree calls for six years of study. Brazilian universities also offer many postgraduate programs.

More and more young Brazilians prefer learning a trade instead of seeking a college degree. Funding for vocational education has exploded in the last decade. The federal government now runs more than five hundred technical institutes or trade schools throughout the nation, where students can learn to become machinists, electricians, welders, carpenters, and information technology specialists, among other jobs. Rural areas offer vocational schools for agriculture courses. Students often hold a day job while taking classes at night. Even with increased funding, the technical schools usually cannot hire enough instructors or buy all the equipment they need. Analysts say that the country needs two or three times more vocational schools to meet the demand, particularly in health care and computer technology. Nonetheless, in a sluggish economy the practical skills taught at these institutes have been a boon for many young Brazilians. "Having the chance to take a graduate degree here changed my life," says Caio Silva, who trained in industrial automation at a technical school in São Paulo. "Everything I have in my professional life is down to this institute."[21]

A Troubled Education System

On average, college graduates earn 2.5 times as much as those with no degrees and five times as much as those who fail to finish secondary school. Part of the reason for this success is that only 11 percent of the working-age population has a degree, making it a mark of distinction. College graduates in Brazil are more likely to be white and wealthy, although that is changing as private, for-profit colleges are beginning to attract large numbers of ethnically diverse students.

Between 2000 and 2012 Brazil achieved amazing drops in illiteracy, from 16.3 million to 13.2 million. But since then improvement has stalled. Nearly one-fifth of the population remains functionally illiterate—able to recognize words and numbers but not able to read and comprehend a sentence. Even more troubling is the level of functional illiteracy among Brazilian youth. According to the Instituto Paulo Montenegro, 38 percent of undergraduates can barely read. These statistics exist despite government programs like Bolsa Família designed to improve education by increasing spending. Experts blame poor planning and educational methods for the problems. Brazil continues to see high dropout rates of about one-third, and high rates of repeating grades. "To foster a healthy, educated workforce, policy makers must make more investments in effective education methods," says Brazilian economist Lindsay Sandoval. "Brazil spends about the same percentage of GDP [gross domestic product] on public education as other Latin American countries; however, gross inefficiencies in the education system undermine this investment."[22]

Failures in the education system lead to continuing problems with inequality in Brazilian society. This is reflected in the competition between public and private schools. About 20 percent of Brazilian youth attend private schools, including most of the upper-middle-class and middle-class children in big cities. Although private schools charge tuition fees that can be exorbitant, free public schools are often crowded and rundown. Parents with little money strive to get their kids into private schools by way of scholarships or limited government subsidies. Education experts say that, on average, students at private schools are academically three years ahead of those in public schools. Despite calls for change, public schools continue to suffer from teacher shortages, heavy workloads, classrooms that are ramshackle and overcrowded, a lack of supplies, and issues with drugs and violence among students. "The great majority of teachers have a lot of good will," says Cleriston Izidro dos Anjos, a professor of education in Brazil. "But work conditions, low salaries, poor training—these are a series of other elements that [don't] allow the work to be done."[23] In addition, permissive laws allow teachers to promote failing students to the next grade, which creates even more distrust in the public system.

> "The great majority of teachers have a lot of good will. But work conditions, low salaries, poor training—these are a series of other elements that [don't] allow the work to be done."[23]
>
> —Cleriston Izidro dos Anjos, a professor of education in Brazil

Anxiety About Jobs

Young Brazilians often seek their first job as an adult in industry or service sectors in large cities. Yet the recent downward spiral in the nation's economy and the resulting rise in unemployment have many first-time job seekers fretting about their future. College graduates are scrambling to get jobs as waiters or hotel staff workers just to survive.

Even middle-class families are feeling the pinch. Joao Vitor Martin Pereira, who is finishing secondary school in the city of Jales in São Paulo state, has watched members of his extended family lose their jobs as unemployment has soared. One cousin was laid off at a meat processing plant and another lost his position installing air conditioners. An aunt who used to have a good job in public health now cleans houses to eke out a living. Pereira's mother, who is a trained nurse, was laid off at a prestigious cancer hospital and now provides home health care for a fraction of what she used to make. In this environment, his father's job as a bank clerk no longer seems so secure. Pereira fears the job market will

A Brazilian restaurant server struggles with a heavily laden tray. Brazil's foundering economy has forced many college-educated Brazilians to turn to service jobs like these to earn a living.

be just as dismal when he is ready to start his career. "Everyone who hasn't already been laid off is pretty much afraid of being laid off," he says. "Everyone there is scared. . . . Despite all that, I think we're still pretty well off compared to the rest of the country."[24]

Street Vendors

Brazilian youths who abandon school early scramble to make a living in the large coastal cities. Many who come from the favelas turn to the informal street economy, operating just outside the margins of the law. Among these are *camelôs*, or street vendors, who commonly are found displaying their wares on sidewalks, parking lots, and beaches. Much of what they sell is cheaply made, such as sunglasses, sarongs, umbrellas, and beach bags. They

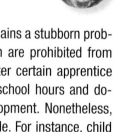

Child Labor in Brazil

Despite the Brazilian government's efforts to stop child labor, it remains a stubborn problem in many parts of the country. Children younger than sixteen are prohibited from working under Brazilian law, although fourteen-year-olds can enter certain apprentice programs. There are also laws against children working during school hours and doing work that may hinder their physical, mental, or social development. Nonetheless, there are millions of underage children working illegally nationwide. For instance, child labor persists in remote areas like the northeast of Brazil, where family farms employ an estimated eight hundred thousand children. Children as young as age ten also work as domestic servants or at markets carrying customers' groceries in wheelbarrows.

Certain cultural norms in Brazil support the use of child labor. Some families insist that children need to learn to work at an early age and do their part to help pay bills. However, José Adilson Pereira da Costa, a prosecutor for the Ministry of Labor, argues that starting to work too soon actually leads to continued poverty. "The child who works since early years repeats the cycle of poverty and will repeat it again with their family," says Costa. "They will have poor school performance, they will not be able to hold good positions in the labor market. The cycle can only be broken with a minimal support for families so that children do not have to work."

Quoted in Sumaia Villela, "Despite Strict Laws, Child Labor in Brazil Is Not Going Away," *Brazzil*, August 11, 2016. http://brazzil.com.

also hawk items that are illegal to sell, including pirated CDs, DVDs, and video games, and knockoffs of brand-name goods. Dealing strictly in cash, these young vendors can appear and disappear quickly. Usually police officers leave them alone unless they receive complaints from jilted customers or annoyed local businesses. Certain young *camelôs* are simply joining the family business. One reporter describes young street vendors in Porto Alegre:

> "Although the older *camelôs* wanted their children to be able to read and to write correctly, they recounted with pride how they had taught them a trade, and thus improved their own economic situation."[25]
>
> —A Brazilian reporter on street vendors in Porto Alegre

As I walked the long corridor between the stalls at different times of the day, I noticed that many of the *camelôs* were aged between 15 and 25 years. Many of them were the children of *camelôs* who had left school early to devote themselves to the family business. Although the older *camelôs* wanted their children to be able to read and to write correctly, they recounted with pride how they had taught them a trade, and thus improved their own economic situation.[25]

In the current economic climate it can be a struggle to survive from day to day. Government promises of better schools and more jobs are shrugged off amid stories of bribery and corruption. And yet, as seen so often with Brazilians, the *camelôs* and other young people in the favelas approach life with spirit and good cheer.

CHAPTER FOUR

Social Life and Culture

Young Brazilians are as passionate about their favorite pop singers and film stars as fans anywhere in the world. Yet when it comes to seeing their idols in person, they feel left out compared to fans in the United States or Europe. So they urge today's headliners like Beyoncé or Bono to make their way to Rio or São Paulo in addition to performing concerts in New York's Central Park or London's Wembley Stadium. This has resulted in the ubiquitous tagline on Twitter: "Come to Brazil." The phrase first gained attention in 2009 when Canadian singer Justin Bieber opened a Twitter account, becoming one of the first major stars to communicate with his fans this way. Tens of thousands of young Brazilians tweeted their urgent invitation: Come to Brazil—in fact, so frequently that it became a popular meme worldwide. Today the request repeatedly turns up on Facebook and YouTube as well. "Look in the replies to any tweet or video from any pop star or teen idol, and you will see the most recognizable phrase on celebrity Internet," says Brian Feldman, an entertainment writer for *New York* magazine. "Dani, a Brazilian Twitter user who regularly asks celebrities . . . to come to Brazil, put it to me simply: 'Brazilian fans do that because we want our idols in Brazil.'"[26] Like Dani, young Brazilians on social media express their hopes that someday soon international stars such as Adele or Drake will be performing to a packed soccer stadium in Rio or São Paulo.

Teenagers and Social Media

A favorite pastime of Brazilian teens is checking up on pop stars and new movies on Internet sites such as Omelete, Judão, and Jovem Nerd. With school lasting only about four hours daily, young people in Brazil—those without after-school jobs—have plenty of time to spend online. And they also tend to be savvy about trends in technology and social media. In fact middle- and upper-class Brazilian teens have the highest user rates for computers and mobile devices of any segment of the population.

A 2013 survey by the Brazilian Center of Studies on Information and Technology showed that teenagers in Brazil regularly used the Internet during the day from various locations. About 40 percent connected while at school, 45 percent connected while on the move, and 70 percent accessed the Internet at home. They

Two Brazilian teens take a break to check social media on their phones. Among Brazilians, middle- and upper-class young people have the highest usage rates of mobile devices.

also employed a variety of devices, from desktop computers and smartphones, which are used most frequently, to notebooks and tablets. The use of multiple devices makes Brazilian teens a prime target for online advertisers and e-commerce sites, which crave the attention of all these avid consumers. Credit card company research shows that Brazilians from age thirteen to eighteen tend to spend all their available money, whether from jobs or allowances, in the short term. More than three-quarters of Brazilian teens are likely to buy things on impulse.

Like teenagers around the world, young Brazilians also love to watch videos online. More than 40 percent view videos every day, and almost half watch them at least twice a week. Favorite videos include comedy clips, dance routines, gaming recommendations, and schoolwork tutorials. Youths also search for videos that suit their particular interests. Soccer enthusiasts might search for videos of Pelé, the legendary Brazilian star of the 1960s, or Ronaldo, the Brazilian player who from 2006 until 2014 held the record in career goals in World Cup play. Black teens in São Paulo have developed a passion for African American gospel music. They watch videos by the hour of black church choirs in the United States, and they compare the voice of Brazilian Robson Nascimento to gospel-influenced singers like Stevie Wonder. Michael Santiago, who now directs a choir at a church in São Paulo, says that watching videos was his chief inspiration: "It was like a thunderbolt. The pastor showed it [the video] to our singing group. I sat there and watched those [African American singers] in that church, and my heart was racing. I broke into a sweat. I never felt like that before. I knew from that day that that was what I had to do with my life."[27]

> "The pastor showed it [the video] to our singing group. I sat there and watched those [African American singers] in that church, and my heart was racing. I broke into a sweat. I never felt like that before. I knew from that day that that was what I had to do with my life."[27]
>
> —Michael Santiago, a choir director at a church in São Paulo

Social networks also attract lots of young Brazilians, with 90 percent of Internet users maintaining profiles on Facebook, Snapchat, Twitter, and other outlets. Two-thirds of these users check

46

the sites daily and respond to the ads included there. Although ordinary news sites receive little teenage traffic in Brazil, blogs like Tumblr enable teens to share their views about school, work, fashion, and current events.

Nightlife and Raves

Teens on social media in Brazil love to discuss the party scene. Nightlife consumes a good deal of a teenager's time and money, especially in large cities. Young people from less-than-wealthy households often take a part-time job after school to help pay for their partying habits. Young people in Brazil live at home longer

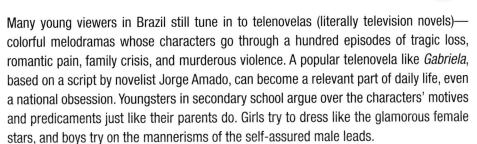

A Surprising Source of Social Progress

Many young viewers in Brazil still tune in to telenovelas (literally television novels)—colorful melodramas whose characters go through a hundred episodes of tragic loss, romantic pain, family crisis, and murderous violence. A popular telenovela like *Gabriela*, based on a script by novelist Jorge Amado, can become a relevant part of daily life, even a national obsession. Youngsters in secondary school argue over the characters' motives and predicaments just like their parents do. Girls try to dress like the glamorous female stars, and boys try on the mannerisms of the self-assured male leads.

Telenovelas can also be a surprising source of social progress. Since the early 2000s, telenovelas have tackled themes of racism, poverty, homosexuality, gay marriage, religious conflict, and abortion. A character in the award-winning *Caminho das Indias* (*India: A Love Story*) struggled with mental illness. Bringing attention to these issues can change viewpoints in society. "They broke the traditional mold," says Carolina Acosta-Alzuru, an associate journalism professor at the University of Georgia. "Brazilians brought in the importance of the context of the story—the ability to say we can say something about society while we tell a love story. I think they really moved the genre up." Acosta-Alzuru adds that the writers must tread a fine line with controversial topics if they want to hold viewers' interest. "If they feel they are being lectured, they will switch channels," she says.

Quoted in Matthew Knight, "Melodramas with a Message," CNN, September 6, 2010. www.cnn.com.

than in years past, and males usually remain longer than females. Nonetheless, teenagers who live at home still have a lot of independence in their social life. Parents in Brazil tend to be lenient with their older children and allow them to stay out later at night. One result is that some teenagers regularly go to late-night parties called raves.

Raves take place outdoors on the beach or in vacant fields or indoors at nightclubs or private houses. Some raves last for an entire weekend. They attract legions of young people crowded into a dark setting with swirling colored lights and booming electronic dance music programmed by a professional disc jockey. Dancing at a rave often goes on for hours.

A Gift for Friendship

The frenzy of the rave scene is only part of the social culture for young Brazilians. In their spare time, many young Brazilians prefer the simpler pleasures of hanging out with friends. Every city or town has its favorite spots for young people to get together. These places, called *pontos de encontro* (meeting points), include parks, town squares, shopping areas, movie theaters, popular street corners, or snack bars where ice cream and soft drinks are served. Many cities close off major streets at night and on weekends so that pedestrians, cyclists, and roller skaters can circulate. Coastal towns offer beautiful beaches as gathering places both day and night. Teenagers flock to these areas to gossip, trade stories and jibes, and argue about movies, music, sports, and telenovelas.

Young people in Brazil have a special gift for friendship, and they pursue it with gusto and good humor. They stay connected with friends via text messages and social media. As soon as someone makes a new acquaintance, he or she will immediately ask for the person's Twitter handle or Instagram address. Brazilian teens also love to bestow nicknames on new friends. "A normal friend will call you by your actual name," says Valeria Almeida, who blogs about Brazil and its customs. "A Brazilian friend will give you a nickname instantly based on what makes you unique. And every Brazilian you'll meet will have a nickname and a real name and you'll have to memorize both."[28] Friendships tend to proceed quickly among young people in Brazil. As Almeida notes,

Like teens everywhere, these Brazilian young people like to just hang out with friends. And in the coastal cities, of course, the beach is always a favorite spot to meet.

a teenager thinks nothing of inviting someone he or she has met five minutes before to come to the family home for pizza, lasagna, or the national specialty of *arroz com feijao* (rice and beans). New friends chatter happily at each other in loud voices as they share thoughts about every topic imaginable.

Music, Television, and Literature

One favorite topic for young Brazilians is music. Teens in Brazil love music, and their country is known for the African-influenced rhythms in its popular music, from samba to bossa nova. Cities like Rio and São Paulo hold drumming competitions throughout the year. Everyone is expected to dance. "You better have some

The Brazilian Way

Brazilians tend to take a relaxed approach to life. They figure that the key to good living is enjoying family and friends and that almost any crisis can be overcome with a smile and a sudden inspiration. This attitude is expressed in the well-known phrase *jeitinho brasileiro*—the Brazilian way of doing things. Something of this could be seen in preparations for the 2016 Olympic Games in Rio. As deadlines approached for the construction of sites and facilities, local officials and workers mostly refused to worry. They assumed that a flurry of last-minute effort would save the day.

For more tightly wound visitors from the United States or Europe, *jeitinho brasileiro* can be exasperating. In restaurants young Brazilians dawdle around the table, and the waitperson is in no hurry to bring the check. Cab drivers will casually round a bill up or down to avoid too much calculation. Pedestrians will stroll ever so slowly on downtown sidewalks. "Speaking to Brazilians about the difference, they prefer their way of living," says Nicolas Lake, an exchange student from Georgetown University.

They appreciate the more casual approach their culture finds normal, and do not get frustrated spending time on everyday tasks. There is even undoubtedly a certain pride that exists among Brazilians over their unique *jeitinho*, knowing that at any time they can walk to one of the many street-side bars, start a conversation, and feel comfortable talking for as long as they please.

Nicolas Lake, "The Brazilian Way: Jeitinho Brasileiro," Berkley Center for Religion, Peace & World Affairs, Georgetown University, December 12, 2014. https://berkleycenter.georgetown.edu.

rhythm or your Brazilian love will teach you all those dances with the passion he has and you cannot fail," says Renate Rigters, a young blogger. "The last thing you want is that you make a fool out of yourself on the dance floor."[29] However, instead of the old forms of popular music, youths today prefer American rap and the catchy pop songs by Brazilian artists that they hear on the radio.

When not online or listening to music, teenagers watch lots of television. Telenovelas, or Brazilian soap operas, have long been a major part of daily life for the young and old of all social classes. These nighttime dramas feature the most lurid story lines and romantic entanglements. Increasing numbers of young people are drawn to American sitcoms. Soccer broadcasts and game shows are popular as well.

Regardless of the literacy rate, reading is not a favorite activity among Brazilian youths. Homes in Brazil are much more likely to have a big-screen television than stuffed bookshelves. Still, there are plenty of books that appeal to young readers' love of adventure and fantasy. For example, Ana Maria Machado's *From Another World* deals with a young man who renovates an old house only to encounter the ghost of a slave girl from the nineteenth century. The novel combines a spine-tingling ghost story with a history lesson about Brazil's slavery period.

Sports as Social Activities

Young Brazilians often set aside their schoolbooks for a soccer ball or some other form of sports equipment. Sports not only provide exercise but also serve as important social activities. Whereas sports programs at school are aimed at promoting fitness, club teams for soccer or volleyball offer competition and the chance to make new friends. Players develop their own social networks in the cities. Young people of all ages play soccer on the beach, in vacant lots, and on manicured fields. In the favelas and rundown neighborhoods, kids often play barefoot on asphalt parking lots and in the street. For an underprivileged teen, the chance to join a youth soccer club can be a ticket out of the slums. The best players get to train with professionals as part of a nationwide system for developing talent. But the clubs also help kids at risk in other ways. "It's not just the money," says Elizandra da Silva, whose son is trying out with a prestigious club team in São Paulo. "This helps them get off the streets, where there are drugs and violence, to try for something better."[30] Like nearly everyone in the country, young people in Brazil also follow the latest exploits of the national soccer team with a dedication that borders on obsession. Both males and females consider themselves experts, and they can spend hours discussing with friends the finer points of the last televised match.

> "It's not just the money. This helps them get off the streets, where there are drugs and violence, to try for something better."[30]
>
> —Elizandra da Silva, whose son is trying out for a club soccer team in São Paulo

Dating in Brazil

As with teenagers almost everywhere, a key part of social life for young Brazilians is dating. Despite Brazil's freewheeling reputation for openness and sexual freedom, rituals for dating and courtship remain rather old-fashioned for many teens. Dating begins in the early to middle teen years and usually consists of casual meetings and gatherings with friends at clubs or cafés. A couple might also take in a movie or concert or stroll to the beach to watch the sunset. Clothing for a date is casual but not sloppy, with males wearing a T-shirt and jeans and females a blouse and jeans or a light dress. In coastal cities with beaches and year-round warm temperatures, tank tops, shorts, and sandals might be worn. Parents generally have few rules about their children's clothes. However, it is considered rude to show up for a date underdressed or in shabby attire. Teens in Brazil take their fashion cues from Europe, and most take pains to look stylish in an offhand way.

> "Conversation is an art there and connections can make or break you, even in Portuguese, there are endless ways (phrases/expressions) to talk about talking."[31]
>
> —A blogger on Brazilian social customs

Brazilians tend to be outgoing even with strangers, so breaking the ice on a first date is usually not a problem. Socializing remains a thriving national pastime. As one Brazilian blogger explains, "Conversation is an art there and connections can make or break you, even in Portuguese, there are endless ways (phrases/expressions) to talk about talking. Things that take away from the chance to connect with someone are not highly regarded."[31] Many couples meet in dance clubs, where inhibitions are few.

Teens in Brazil like to flirt and are comfortable when crowded together in tight spaces. They are far from shy about making eye contact and poking fun at new acquaintances. According to one teen on an online forum,

> Brazilians like eye contact and it's not seen as a faux pas [social mistake] like in some cultures. A Brazilian girl while talking to you will often stare right at your eyes and into your soul, for long periods . . . it's totally normal. . . . They have a great sense of humor too and Brazilians will laugh a

lot with each other in social gatherings. They may make a little fun of you and others too, but it's all very lighthearted and they don't intend to hurt your feelings. They like having a good laugh.[32]

Brazilian youths regard casual touching as friendly and natural. Young women greet others, even strangers, with a kiss on both cheeks, and males hug each other as a matter of course. Foreign visitors are often struck by the way young women in Brazil will sign their e-mails to new acquaintances with *beijos* (kisses). Brazilians can also be casual about showing off their bodies. Their famous beaches are filled with women of all ages wearing swimsuits that are barely more than artfully arranged strings.

For Brazilian teens, dating is often a casual affair, such as gathering with friends at cafés, clubs, or other local hangouts.

Despite family lectures about abstinence, teenagers regularly have sex before marriage. With extended families living together in one household, couples can have trouble finding privacy in either young person's home. However, they are usually resourceful in getting around this problem. Old gender norms are changing, but they dictate that males may have several partners prior to marriage, but females are expected to have only one or two, if any. Brazilians today are more likely to accept premarital sex and living together outside marriage. School sex education programs have been successful in promoting the use of condoms among teenagers. This is a welcome development, as Brazil has long had one of the highest rates of teenage pregnancy in the world. Brazil has nearly as many births among women ages fifteen to nineteen as among those twenty-five to twenty-nine. Experts view teen pregnancy as one of the main causes of income inequality, high unemployment, and persistent poverty in the country.

> "Brazilians like eye contact . . . A Brazilian girl while talking to you will often stare right at your eyes and into your soul, for long periods."[32]
>
> —A teen commenting in an online forum

Engagement and Marriage

For middle- and upper-class Brazilians, the period of courtship and engagement can last for months and sometimes even years. In traditional families, the young man will ask his girlfriend's father for permission to marry her. "There are some couples that like to wear rings when they are dating," notes Ana Gabriela Verotti Farah, a Brazilian writer. "In these cases, the ring is called [a] promise ring—in Brazil, *anel de compromisso* or commitment ring—and is usually made of silver or steel. These kinds of rings are usually equal for both and it is important in these cases that the couple's rings are the same style."[33] During this courtship time the young people may live apart in their respective family homes or, increasingly, find cheap lodgings of their own. If they decide to get married, the couple may arrange for two weddings—a legal civil ceremony before a judge and a religious ceremony to be attended by family and friends.

Brazilian culture does not lack for wedding day traditions. For example, it is customary for the bride to wear gold heels. She writes the names of her single girlfriends inside the hem of her dress to give them good luck in finding a husband. Bridesmaids are expected to wear dresses of different colors—never the same—and bright colors are preferred. And after the ceremony everyone indulges in eating, drinking, and dancing. The bride will slip off her gold shoes and place them in the middle of the dance floor so guests can toss money into the shoes. The celebration usually extends deep into the night. As with so many examples of social life in Brazil, the wedding atmosphere is filled with voices, laughter, and music.

CHAPTER FIVE

Religious Life

The worshippers tread along dirt roads leading to the small chapel at 5:30 every morning. Most are young, with an average age in the mid-twenties. At first they listen to a guitarist strumming a sacred melody and singing with passion. Then everyone joins in, raising their voices in a mixture of languages, making what they experience as a joyful noise. Soon the people are singing in tongues, creating their own words that flow together in a spontaneous chorus. This service is one of many held each day at Canção Nova, a Catholic retreat located in Cachoeira Paulista, a small community in the state of São Paulo. Father Robert J. Carr, a visiting priest, sees Canção Nova as the future of Catholicism. "We [are] all united in our singing of praise and in our lack of knowledge of what we are saying," he declares. "We just know it is joyous, and we feel spiritually strengthened. I fit in with the other worshippers of God for only this moment because this is Brazil."[34] Carr believes that the services at Canção Nova appeal to young people in ways that the traditional church cannot.

A Variety of Religions and Beliefs

Brazil is home to a variety of religions and spiritual beliefs among young and old. Surveys show that 90 percent of Brazilians hold some form of religious belief. Brazil is the most religious nation in South America, with Catholicism the dominant faith by far. An estimated 123 million Roman Catholics live in Brazil, the highest total of any nation. The statue of Christ the Redeemer atop Mount Corcovado that has loomed over Rio de Janeiro since 1931 has become one of the nation's most recognizable religious symbols.

Despite Catholicism's dominant place in Brazilian society, the share of the population that considers itself Catholic has been in steep decline for several decades, falling from 92 percent in

1970 to 65 percent in 2010, the last year of the Brazilian census. A survey by the polling institute Datafolha shows a loss of about 9 million practicing Catholics since 2014. At the same time, the number of Protestants has been growing, from 26 million in 2000 to more than 42 million in 2010. The segment of the population who professes some other faith or no organized religion at all is also on the rise.

The huge statue of Christ the Redeemer looming over the city of Rio de Janeiro is one of the city's most recognizable sights. Brazil has the highest number of Roman Catholics of any nation.

Young people are driving this change in Brazil's spiritual life. From 1970 to 2010 the percentage of fifteen- to twenty-nine-year-olds who think of themselves as Catholic has fallen by almost one-third. At the same time, the percentage of Protestants in this age range has gone up from 5 percent to 22 percent. A significant number of young Brazilians are moving to Pentecostal, Methodist, or other Protestant churches, and some are not attending services altogether. (Pentecostal churches emphasize personal experience of God, including baptism in the Holy Spirit and faith healing.) This shift in belief patterns, especially the movement toward secular beliefs, continues to affect all aspects of life in Brazil, particularly social mores and politics.

The Daily Life of a Young Catholic

Nonetheless, for many young Brazilians the Catholic faith remains the centerpiece of their lives. Children raised in a devout family might attend Mass every day, either early in the morning or in the late afternoon. Some older youths assist the clergy during Mass as altar servers. For boys, this can be a way of training for the priesthood. Many children gather with their family to say the rosary at an altar in their home each day before school. The rosary is a set of formal prayers to Jesus and Mary that is recited while holding a string of knots or beads pertaining to the number of prayers. A child might also say the rosary on a school bus or during a break between classes. The sight of young people praying in public is very common in Brazil. For some this may be only a routine they follow, without deep conviction. "Without a doubt, countless church facades and passengers praying on rosaries are sights I commonly witness when riding the bus to school each morning," says Alanna Hughes, a young Catholic visitor to São Paulo. "Yet, I have not met many people who admit to skipping a soccer game or shopping trip to make sure they catch a homily [Catholic sermon]."[35]

Some young Brazilians attend Catholic schools, which are numerous in the nation. These are privately run institutions that

> "I have not met many people who admit to skipping a soccer game or shopping trip to make sure they catch a homily [Catholic sermon]."[35]
>
> —Alanna Hughes, a young Catholic visitor to São Paulo

Catholic Leaders and the Zika Virus

In May 2015 the Zika virus began its alarming spread in Brazil and Latin America. More than 1.5 million people have been infected since the outbreak, usually through mosquito bites or sexual activity. Women infected with the Zika virus run a severe risk should they become pregnant because the virus can cause severe birth defects, including an abnormally small head and underdeveloped brain. News of this danger has led health experts to recommend that Brazilian women of childbearing age use some form of birth control. Nonetheless, despite the risks, Catholic bishops in Brazil have resisted condoning the use of contraception, even on a temporary basis, because Catholic doctrine regards using birth control as a sin.

The crisis also has brought Brazil's strict abortion laws into the limelight. Abortion advocates are urging government officials to relax the laws in order to prevent births of babies with severe microcephaly, or unnaturally small heads and brains. Activists in Brazil are outraged that Catholic officials refuse to budge from their stance against abortion. "The fears over the Zika virus are giving us a rare opening to challenge the religious fundamentalists who put the lives of thousands of women at risk in Brazil each year to maintain laws belonging in the Dark Ages," says Silvia Camurca, director of SOS Corpo, a feminist group in Recife. The protests led Evangelical politicians to consider making abortion laws tougher—instead of more accommodating—demonstrating the heated emotions this controversy continues to stir.

Quoted in Joan Frawley Desmond, "Brazilian Bishops Reject Abortion as Zika Response," *National Catholic Register*, February 16, 2016. www.ncregister.com.

---

include some religious instruction but also accept pupils of other religions. "There is not a cross in every classroom or fathers who teach classes," reports one visiting student at a Catholic school. "The fact that there is a chapel on campus and a large cross in the center of the courtyard makes up for this—physical reminders that students attend a Catholic institution."[36] Private Catholic schools are considered to be academically among the best in Brazil.

Celebrating Milestones in a Catholic Life

For children in traditional Catholic families, there are stages of development in the faith that align with sacraments. Baptism is the first and most fundamental sacrament. Most Catholics are baptized as infants, when a priest will sprinkle holy water on the baby's head. This symbolizes the washing away of sin and entry into the Roman Catholic Church. First Communion, in which a Catholic child first receives the wafer and wine that represent the body and blood of Christ, usually occurs between the ages of seven and thirteen. Confirmation, when the young person is sealed with the Holy Spirit and enters the Catholic faith as a mature soul, is a rite of passage to adulthood that takes place around age fourteen. These sacraments are often celebrated with ribbons, candles, prayers, and a large dinner that includes the extended family.

A girl's fifteenth birthday and her entry into womanhood is marked with a celebration called *festa de debutantes* (party of debutantes) or *festa de quinze anos* (party of fifteen years). It is the equivalent of the *quinceañera* in other Catholic cultures. Celebrations vary from family to family, but most include a Mass followed by dancing, an elaborate meal, cake cutting, and the presentation of a video about the girl's life. The *festa* once was the first opportunity for an inexperienced girl to meet and mingle with young males, but it now represents her first chance to be the center of an adult-style party and wear makeup, jewelry, and high heels. Wealthy families sometimes spend enormous amounts on a daughter's *festa de quinze anos*, but some Brazilian females, such as the sociologist/blogger Brasilmagic, reject the tradition as old-fashioned:

> When I turned 15, I was living in Brazil and I knew I did not want a lavish party. I was skeptical of the whole idea of being introduced to society. At the age of 15, I was still a kid. . . . Several decades later, the 15th birthday tradition seems sexist and backwards as ever. It's from a time when women were married off to desirable men at a very young age. It's from a time when women had few options in life other than get married and have babies.[37]

Marriage is also a sacrament in Catholicism. Young couples who choose to have a Catholic wedding usually must take a one-day course before the ceremony that helps prepare them for the ebb and flow of a lifelong marriage and reaffirms their faith. The ceremony itself is marked by sacred traditions. "The bride will usually also walk into the church with [the song] Ave Maria playing," notes a Brazilian blogger named Polyana. "At the church, there is the signing of the marriage license, and it is also signed by padrinhos and padrinhas, the North American equivalent of the wedding party."[38] Marriage parties in Brazil tend to be marathon affairs featuring plenty of food, drink, music of all kinds, and dancing.

Controversial Doctrines

Despite the survival of church traditions, there are signs that Catholic belief is waning among the young in Brazil. One indication is the nation's fertility rate. At 1.76 children per female, it has fallen below the replacement rate and stands as one of the lowest rates in Latin America. Experts predict this will mean fewer children becoming baptized and confirmed, fewer young prospects to become priests and nuns, and fading connections between parents and the Catholic Church. The trend has become so pronounced that Cardinal Cláudio Hummes, one of the main

Brazilian Catholics attend Mass during a holiday celebration. Many young Brazilians are ignoring the conservative teachings of the Catholic Church, especially regarding sexuality.

Catholic leaders in Brazil, is beginning to question the future for his church: "We wonder with anxiety: how long will Brazil remain a Catholic country?"[39]

Brazilian teenagers seem to be chafing against the conservative doctrines of the Catholic Church—when they are not ignoring them altogether. The church's positions on sexual matters and reproductive rights seem out of touch with the daily reality for many young people. Low birth rates show that young women in Brazil are turning to artificial methods of contraception, the use of which the Catholic Church forbids as sinful. During the 1980s, as a result of public opinion and the growing women's movement,

Blurring the Sacred and Secular

Many of Brazil's festivals and holidays are based on Catholic traditions, even when the religious aspect of the celebration has faded. "When celebrated as festivals, feasts often blur boundaries between sacred and secular," explains the website Catholics & Cultures, "and at times, as has often been said of Catholic countries' Carnival festivals, [make] legitimate the ritual overturning of social conventions for a short period of time." Indeed, Carnival in Brazil is recognized as one of the wildest celebrations in the world. It is a weeklong party to mark the end of the period before Lent, the forty-day observance of abstinence and sacrifice before Easter. Revelers in masks and outlandish—and often skimpy—costumes ride atop elaborate floats and dance in the streets until late in the night. The Carnival celebration in Rio bears the influence of the favelas, with groups of youths from the neighborhood samba schools putting on dazzling dance performances. Hundreds of bands march through the streets blaring a variety of musical styles as huge papier-mâché figures bob atop the swirling crowds. Carnival celebrations in other parts of Brazil take on the flavor of the local culture. For example, in the northeast region of Bahia, African influences add a distinctive rhythm to the reggae and samba music and dancing. Indigenous groups dressed in tribal costumes contribute their own unique local flavor to the proceedings.

Catholics & Cultures, "Feasts, Processions & Festivals." www.catholicsandcultures.org.

the Ministry of Health began to offer family planning services as part of an overall program for women's health. The 1997 Family Planning Law allowed for sterilization of women through the public health network and made birth control pills available over the counter. Since then, information about different kinds of contraception has become widely available, and young women of all social classes now have access to them.

Today more than 80 percent of Brazilian women of childbearing age use some form of contraception, including condoms, birth control pills, and even the controversial morning-after pills, which are used to prevent pregnancy after unprotected sex. In a country considered a bastion of the Catholic faith, this development has been startling. Susana Cruzalta, writing on the blog *Catholics for Choice*, sees changing social attitudes among many young Catholics in Brazil:

> Most of the young people I spoke with said they do not see a conflict between their faith and contraception or premarital sex. Rafaela, a 19-year-old girl from Rio, said she hopes that all cardinals and bishops worldwide follow the pope's steps and come down to the level of the people, especially by reaching out to young people, who are a majority in Latin American countries. She said she disagrees with church teachings on sexuality and is convinced she is not a bad Catholic because she has had sex before marriage and takes the pill. Rafaela said she wishes that the [Catholic] hierarchy would look at contraception and abortion as public health issues.[40]

Abortion and Gay Rights

Views about abortion are changing as well, although much more slowly. The Catholic Church, which forbids abortion, has used its political clout to keep abortion from becoming legal. In fact, Brazil has some of the world's most restrictive abortion laws. Large majorities in the Brazilian Congress strongly oppose the procedure. Among the people, 65 percent agree with the ban, with only 16 percent against it.

Despite the ban, abortion is not uncommon. The Ministry of Health estimates that more than 1 million abortions are performed in the country each year. More than two hundred thousand young women are hospitalized each year from complications connected to getting an illegal abortion, including dangerous infections and vaginal bleeding. Experts say that most women who seek out illegal abortions are young, poor, and uneducated. A 2010 study found that 42 percent of women get their first abortion between ages twelve and nineteen. The study also determined that among women with less than a fourth-grade education, 23 percent have had an abortion. The health risks of getting an illegal abortion are much greater for lower-income Brazilian teens in the favelas and other impoverished areas, says Carmen Barroso, the regional director of the International Planned Parenthood Federation in the Western Hemisphere. "If you are older and you have money, there are private clinics that are reasonably good," notes Barroso. "But if you are young and poor, you are really at the mercy of this terrible situation."[41]

> "If you are older and you have money, there are private [abortion] clinics that are reasonably good. But if you are young and poor, you are really at the mercy of this terrible situation."[41]
>
> —Carmen Barroso, regional director of the International Planned Parenthood Federation in the Western Hemisphere

In contrast to its abortion laws, Brazil's laws regarding gay rights are surprisingly liberal. Despite the Catholic Church's doctrine that homosexuality is a sin, the government has moved to support the rights of members of the lesbian, gay, bisexual, and transgender (LGBT) community. Employment discrimination against LGBT individuals was outlawed in 2011, and gay marriage was legalized in 2013. In support of this new liberalization, Pope Francis, the Argentine-born leader of the worldwide Catholic Church, has made remarks defending gay rights. During his 2014 visit to Rio de Janeiro for World Youth Day, the pope told reporters, "If a person is gay, seeks God and has good will, who am I to judge him?"[42] In many ways Brazil has sought to present itself as a gay-friendly country. São Paulo hosts the world's largest gay pride festival, and Carnival is famous for its flamboyant transgender participants.

Flamboyant revelers pose during São Paulo's gay pride celebration, the world's largest. Despite its Roman Catholic–influenced culture, Brazil likes to present itself as a gay-friendly country.

The Rise of the Evangelicals

Increasing numbers of young Brazilians are rejecting the Catholic way of life for other approaches to Christianity. One dramatic change is the growth of Evangelical Protestants—Christians who adhere strictly to biblical teachings and believe they can be born again as followers of Jesus. Some predict that by 2030 the number of Evangelicals in Brazil will equal the number of Catholics. The change is on stark display, for example, in the town square in Rio known as Cinelandia, named for all the movie theaters (or cinemas) that used to reside there. Those theaters have given way to Evangelical chapels with names like the World Church of the Kingdom of God lit up in neon. According to José Eustaquio Alves of the National School of Statistical Science in Rio, "Brazil is unique: It's the only country to have seen such a profound change in its religious landscape in so short a time."[43]

Evangelical ministries in Brazil resort to all sorts of innovative practices to attract young followers and separate themselves from the supposedly stodgy traditional church. "In order to recruit a diverse group of believers, the church has had to experiment with various campaign tactics such as Extreme Fight Night, rock concerts, video games, and on-site tattoo parlors," reports Diana Londono, a research associate at the Council on Hemispheric Affairs. "Furthermore, the rate of conversion would not have been as successful without the use of technology, including outreach via radio and television."[44] Some Brazilian Evangelical leaders promote the power of belief among young people through speaking in tongues, as at Canção Nova, or in faith healing.

> "A majority of evangelicals used to be Catholic, but being a Catholic doesn't mean that you practice the Faith. Conversely, an evangelical is an evangelical at work, in school, in the community."[46]
>
> —Silas Malafaia, a well-known television preacher in Brazil

For example, on Mondays at the International Mission of Miracles, a Pentecostal church in a working-class area outside Rio, poor families arrive to see eleven-year-old Alani Santos. Santos's father, Adauto, built the church, serves as its pastor, and touts his young daughter's healing powers. Visitors hobble to the stage or gather hopefully on crutches and in wheelchairs to receive Alani's touch. After the service one young man with HIV described the encounter: "When she touched me with her hands, it was an inexplicable thing. I felt a good presence, as if my blood was being renewed."[45] Alani also leads Wednesday night services in which she and other pastors predict future events. Saturdays she broadcasts a radio show dealing with the Bible. Alani even conducts healing sessions via Skype to attend to those who cannot make the journey to São Gonçalo.

Such practices attract young believers who were raised in the Catholic Church but have lost connection with the church's teachings. "A majority of evangelicals used to be Catholic, but being a Catholic doesn't mean that you practice the Faith," notes Silas Malafaia, a well-known television preacher in Brazil. "Conversely, an evangelical is an evangelical at work, in school, in the community."[46] It remains to be seen how these profound changes in Brazil's spiritual landscape will affect future generations of its young people. What is certain is that overwhelming numbers of young Brazilians are determined to make their own decisions about religious belief and daily spiritual life.

SOURCE NOTES

Chapter One: A Rich Cultural Mix

1. Quoted in Liv Siddall, "Brazil's Creative Culture: Six Creatives Tell Us What Makes the South American Country So Inspiring," It's Nice That, June 3, 2015. www.itsnicethat.

2. Quoted in Hayden Bird, "Gisele Gets Emotional Talking About the Destruction of the Brazilian Rainforest," Boston.com, November 15, 2016. www.boston.com.

3. Thiago de Paula Souza, "African Cultural Heritage in Brazil," World Policy Blog, March 31, 2016. www.worldpolicy.org.

4. Quoted in Lulu Garcia-Navarro, "Expats Find Brazil's Reputation for Race-Blindness Is Undone by Reality," National Public Radio, May 22, 2015. www.npr.org.

5. Quoted in Garcia-Navarro, "Expats Find Brazil's Reputation for Race-Blindness Is Undone by Reality."

6. Quoted in Joe Leahy and Samantha Pearson, "Brazil: Tales of Everyday Agony," Financial Times, May 15, 2016. www.ft.com.

7. Quoted in BBC News, "Rio de Janeiro Favela Life Described by Children," December 28, 2015. www.bbc.com.

Chapter Two: Family Life

8. Quoted in Melissa Block, "Brazil's New Middle Class: A Better Life, Not an Easy One," National Public Radio, September 18, 2013. www.npr.org.

9. Quoted in Anne Carolina Ramos, "Children and Intergenerational Relationships: The Relations Between Grandparents and Grandchildren from Children's Perspectives." www.inter-disciplinary.net.

10. Quoted in Huffington Post, "What Brazil Can Teach the World About Living Well," January 28, 2014. www.huffingtonpost.com.

11. Quoted in Quora, "Do Men Do House Chores in Brazil?," September 6, 2015. www.quora.com.

12. Rosana McPhee, "Brazilian Food and Customs," *Foodie Bugle Journal*, May 15, 2011. http://thefoodiebugle.com.

13. Sheila Thomson, "Food & Eating Habits: Breakfast, Lunch & Dinner," Maria-Brazil. www.maria-brazil.org.

14. *Minhas Crônicas do Brasil* (blog), "Bucket Brigade," October 13, 2015. https://cronicasdobrasil.wordpress.com.

15. Quoted in Juan Forero, "Brazil's Falling Birth Rate: A 'New Way of Thinking,'" National Public Radio, January 15, 2012. www.npr.org.

Chapter Three: Education and Employment

16. Elizabeth Bacelar, "'Vestibular' Holds Key to University," *News-Times*, May 10, 2004. www.newstimes.com.

17. Quoted in Larry Rohter, "Rio Journal; For Brazil's College-Bound, a Brutal Test of Mettle," *New York Times*, December 29, 2000. www.nytimes.

18. Quoted in *Time for Kids*, "A Day in the Life: Brazil." www.timeforkids.com.

19. Quoted in Ben Tavener, "Brazil Struggles to Reduce Child Labor," *Rio Times*, June 4, 2013. http://riotimesonline.com.

20. Quoted in Donna Bowater, "Spotlight on Enem Exam in Brazil After Questions Row," *Times Higher Education*, December 3, 2015. www.timeshighereducation.com.

21. Quoted in Andrew Downie, "In Brazil, Vocational Education Expands to Meet Demands of a Booming Economy," *Chronicle of Higher Education*, July 5, 2011. www.chronicle.com.

22. Lindsay Sandoval, "The Effect of Education on Brazil's Economic Development," *Global Majority E-Journal*, vol. 3, no. 1, June 2012. www.american.edu.

23. Quoted in Seth Kugel, "Brazil's Vexing Public Education Problem," Public Radio International, September 20, 2010. www.pri.org.

24. Quoted in Brianna Lee, "Brazil Unemployment Rate Soars as Workers Brace for Tighter Economic Squeeze," *International Business Times*, October 5, 2015. www.ibtimes.com.

25. Diego Coletto, *The Informal Economy and Employment in Brazil: Latin America, Modernization, and Social Changes*. New York: Palgrave Macmillan, 2010, p. 118.

Chapter Four: Social Life and Culture

26. Brian Feldman, "How 'Come to Brazil' Came to the Internet," *New York*, January 28, 2016. http://nymag.com.
27. Quoted in John Burdick, *The Color of Sound: Race, Religion, and Music in Brazil*. New York: New York University Press, 2013, p. 132.
28. Valeria Almeida, "11 Differences Between a Normal Friend and a Brazilian Friend," Matador Network, October 12, 2015. https://matadornetwork.com.
29. Renate Rigters, "7 Reasons Why You Should Never Date a Brazilian," *That Wanderlust* (blog), April 14, 2015. http://that wanderlust.com.
30. Quoted in Lulu Garcia-Navarro, "For Brazil's Soccer Stars, Careers Often Begin on Makeshift Fields," National Public Radio, May 19, 2014. www.npr.org.
31. Tudobeleza, "Socialness Among Brazilians," *Eyes on Brazil* (blog), July 31, 2008. https://eyesonbrazil.wordpress.com.
32. Quoted in Reddit Brazil, "I Am a Little Smitten with a Brazilian Girl. Advice?" www.reddit.com.
33. Ana Gabriela Verotti Farah, "Relationships and Ring Wearing in Brazil," Brazil Business, July 2, 2013. http://thebrazilbusi ness.com.

Chapter Five: Religious Life

34. Robert J. Carr, "Cancao Nova," Catholic Online. www.catho lic.org.
35. Alanna Hughes, "Alanna Hughes on Religion in Daily Life in Brazil," Berkley Center for Religion, Peace & World Affairs, Georgetown University, February 12, 2007. https://berkley center.georgetown.edu.
36. Tevin Simard, "From Catholic School to Catholic School," Berkley Center for Religion, Peace & World Affairs, Georgetown University, March 24, 2017. https://berkleycenter.george town.edu.

37. *Brasilmagic's Weblog*, "The 15th Birthday Party Tradition," May 20, 2010. https://brasilmagic.wordpress.com.

38. Polyana, "Brazilian Wedding Traditions," *Portuguese Language Blog*, July 16, 2010. http://blogs.transparent.com.

39. Quoted in Simon Romero, "A Laboratory for Revitalizing Catholicism," *New York Times*, February 14, 2013. www.nytimes.com.

40. Susana Cruzalta, "Young Brazilians Hope New Pope Will 'Modernize' Church on Social Justice Issues," *Catholics for Choice* (blog), July 30, 2013. www.catholicsforchoice.org.

41. Quoted in Grace Wyler, "What It Is Like to Get an Abortion in Brazil, One of the Most Restrictive Countries in the World," *Business Insider*, May 4, 2013. www.businessinsider.com.

42. Quoted in Jessica Robineau, "Brazil: Homosexuality, Religious Beliefs, and Intolerance," *Le Journal International*, November 24, 2015. www.lejournalinternationale.fr.

43. Quoted in Lamia Oualalou, "Dramatic Religious Shift in Brazil as Evangelicals Are Rapidly Overtaking Catholics," AlterNet, November 3, 2014. www.alternet.org.

44. Diana Londono, "Evangelicals in Brazil," Council on Hemispheric Affairs, December 5, 2012. www.coha.org.

45. Quoted in Samantha M. Shapiro, "The Child Preachers of Brazil," *New York Times*, June 11, 2015. www.nytimes.com.

46. Quoted in Juliana Freitag, "Brazil Loses 9 Million Catholics in 2 Years," Church Militant, January 2, 2017. www.churchmilitant.com.

FOR FURTHER RESEARCH

Books

Juliana Barbassa, *Dancing with the Devil in the City of God: Rio de Janeiro and the Olympic Dream*. New York: Touchstone, 2015.

John Burdick, *The Color of Sound: Race, Religion, and Music in Brazil*. New York: New York University Press, 2013.

R. Ben Penglase, *Living with Insecurity in a Brazilian Favela*. New Brunswick, NJ: Rutgers University Press, 2014.

Michael Reid, *Brazil: The Troubled Rise of a Global Power*. New Haven, CT: Yale University Press, 2016.

Larry Rohter, *Brazil on the Rise*. New York: St. Martin's, 2012.

Internet Sources

Juliana Freitag, "Brazil Loses 9 Million Catholics in 2 Years," Church Militant, January 2, 2017. www.churchmilitant.com/news /article/brazil-loses-9-million-catholics-in-2-years.

Lulu Garcia-Navarro, "For Brazil's Soccer Stars, Careers Often Begin on Makeshift Fields," *National Public Radio*, May 19, 2014. www.npr.org/sections/parallels/2014/05/19/313982248/for-brazils -soccer-stars-careers-often-begin-on-makeshift-fields.

Joe Leahy and Samantha Pearson, "Brazil: Tales of Everyday Agony," *Financial Times*, May 15, 2016. www.ft.com/content/1c0 67b52-1829-11e6-bb7d-ee563a5a1cc1.

Rosana McPhee, "Brazilian Food and Customs," Foodie Bugle Journal, May 15, 2011. http://thefoodiebugle.com/article/cooks /brazilian-food-and-customs.

Stephanie Nolen, "Brazil's Colour Bind," *Globe and Mail*, July 31, 2015. www.theglobeandmail.com/news/world/brazils-colour-bind /article25779474.

Erik Ortiz, "What Is a Favela? Five Things to Know About Rio's So-Called Shantytowns," NBC News, August 4, 2016. www .nbcnews.com/storyline/2016-rio-summer-olympics/what-favela -five-things-know-about-rio-s-so-called-n622836.

Websites

Countries and Their Cultures: Brazil (www.everyculture.com /Bo-Co/Brazil.html). This website, part of the *World Culture Encyclopedia*, provides a good overview of Brazil and its culture, including sections on demography, history and ethnic relations, food and economy, social stratification, and political life.

Indigenous People (Today) (http://sites.jmu.edu/migrationflows /indigenous-tribes-today). This website examines three key aspects of Brazil's indigenous people: their languages, the land they share with the nation, and their prospects for the future.

Minhas Crônicas do Brasil (https://cronicasdobrasil.wordpress .com/about). *Minhas Crônicas do Brasil* is a blog that brings together *crônicas*, or personal journals, from many different young people living and working in Brazil. It is an excellent source for details about daily life in rural and urban sections of the country.

INDEX

PICTURE CREDITS

Cover: iStock.com/AfricaImages

6: Maury Aaseng (map)

6: iStock.com/liangpv (flag)

7: (top to bottom) Lazyllama/Depositphotos.com;
   Mark Schwettmann/Shutterstock.com; joelfotos/
   Depositphotos.com; iStock.com/Rudimencial

9: iStock.com/FernandoPodolski

11: Jean-Paul Chatagnon/Minden Pictures

17: Lazyllama/Shutterstock.com

21: iStock.com/Cesar Okada

25: iStock.com/PurpleImages

29: picture alliance/Sandra Gätke/Newscom

34: Paulo Whitaker/Reuters/Newscom

37: Werner Rudhart/picture alliance/dpa/Newscom

41: Marko Djurica/Reuters/Newscom

45: iStock.com/Rudimencial

49: Gardel Bertrand/ZumaPress/Newscom

53: David R. Frazier/DanitaDelimont.com "Danita Delimont
    Photography"/Newscom

57: Mark Schwettmann/Shutterstock.com

61: alfribeiro/Depositphotos.com

65: MAR Photography/Shutterstock.com

ABOUT THE AUTHOR

John Allen is a writer who lives and works in Oklahoma City.